D0607620

Bear and Roly-Poly

ELIZABETH WINTHROP

ILLUSTRATED BY

PATIENCE BREWSTER

HOLIDAY HOUSE/NEW YORK

For Katherine Cordelia Alsop,
with a big fat hug and an extra squeeze.

E.W.

For Ezmeralda P. Smythe,
whose life and letters I'd be lost without,
and thanks to J.J. Gregg
for his roly-poly size and shape.

P.B.

Printed in the United States of America
First Edition

Library of Congress Cataloging-in-Publication Data
Winthrop, Elizabeth.
Bear and Roly-Poly / Elizabeth Winthrop ; illustrated by Patience Brewster. — 1st ed.
p. cm.
Summary: Bear is happily surprised to learn that Roly-Poly, his baby sister, likes to have him give her attention and even sing her to sleep.
ISBN 0-8234-1197-4
[1. Bears—Fiction. 2. Babies—Fiction. 3. Brothers and sisters—Fiction.] I. Brewster, Patience, ill. II. Title.
PZ7.W768Bdr 1996 95-6069 CIP AC
[E]—dc20

Bear and Roly-Poly

One day, Nora said to Bear, "I'm going over to Grandma's house. She is giving us a present."

"Goody, goody, goody," said Bear. "What is it?"

"A new baby sister," said Nora.

"A baby sister!" Bear cried.

"Yes," said Nora.

She gave Bear a big fat hug and an extra squeeze.

"Here comes Mrs. Duck.
She'll take care of you while I'm gone."

"Nora is going to Grandma's house to get my baby sister," Bear told Mrs. Duck.

"Yes, I know," said Mrs. Duck.

"Your baby sister is very lucky to have a big brother like you."

"I'm going to take good care of her," said Bear.

All afternoon, Bear practiced being a big brother.
He rocked his doll
in the rocking chair.

He gave her a bath
in the sink.

He poured milk into his
old baby bottle and
fed it to her.

He patted her on the back
to make her burp.

Finally Nora came home.
She carried the new baby right into Bear's room.
Bear stared.
Mrs. Duck stared too.
Nobody said anything for a minute.

Then Mrs. Duck said, "Oh, my,"
and Nora said, "Bear, this is Roly-Poly, your baby sister."
"She's not a baby," cried Bear.
"She's almost as big as Mrs. Duck.
And she's not brown like me."
"Babies come in all colors and sizes,"
said Nora.

"Oh," said Bear. "Can I hold her?"
"Sit in the rocking chair," said Nora
and she rested Roly-Poly in his lap.
"She's a very heavy baby," Bear gasped.
Roly-Poly opened her eyes
and looked at Bear.
"Hello," said Bear.
"I'm your big brother."

Roly-Poly opened her mouth
and began to cry.
Nora lifted the baby
off Bear's lap
and rocked her.

"She doesn't like me," Bear said.

"She's going to love you," said Nora.

"Everything is new and strange to her right now," Mrs. Duck said. "Come on, let's make her bed."

So Bear helped make Roly-Poly's bed.

Then he poured milk into her bottle, and Mrs. Duck heated it up.

"I have to go home now," said Mrs. Duck.

She gave the bottle to Nora. "Will you be all right?"

"I have Bear to help me," said Nora.

"Can I feed Roly-Poly?" Bear asked

"Of course," said Nora.

Nora held the enormous baby in her lap, and Bear stood on a chair. He put the bottle in the baby's mouth. Roly-Poly sucked and sucked.

When the milk was all gone, she stared at Bear.

He stared back. "You have soft fur," he said.

Roly-Poly closed her eyes and began to cry.

"She needs to be burped," Nora yelled above the noise. She propped Roly-Poly up on her shoulder. Bear stood on a stool and patted the baby on the back.

"I think you'll have to pat a little harder," cried Nora.

So Bear pounded Roly-Poly between the shoulder blades. Suddenly a great big noisy burp came rolling up out of her stomach.

Roly-Poly stopped crying.

"Good job," said Nora.

"I'm tired," said Bear, as he climbed down from the stool. "Babies are hard work."

"They certainly are," said Nora.

GRAMMA JO
S.H.B.'s
EZMARELDA
MARLEE
MIGHTY
TRACY & SAM
PETUNIA
MARTHA & SAM
HOLLY HERMIMER
MARYANNE
SPRINKEL
KARA & SEB

A few days later, Mrs. Duck came to babysit while Nora went to the store.

As soon as Nora left, Roly-Poly started to cry. Mrs. Duck picked her up and carried her around, but Roly-Poly would not stop crying.

Mrs. Duck tried to feed her, but she wasn't hungry.

Mrs. Duck tried to burp her, but she didn't need to be burped.

Roly-Poly just went right on crying.

Bear climbed into his rocking chair and looked at his books.

"Babies aren't much fun," he said. "They cry a lot."

"Maybe you could sing to her," said Mrs. Duck.

"I don't think so," Bear said. "She doesn't like me."

"Please try, Bear," said Mrs. Duck.

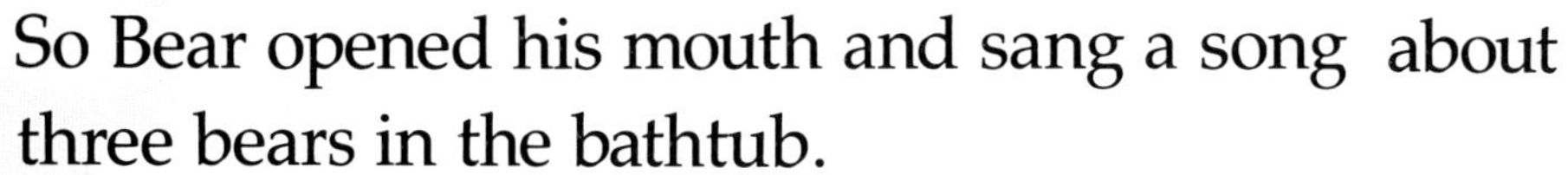

So Bear opened his mouth and sang a song about three bears in the bathtub.

He sang very loud.

Roly-Poly stopped crying for a moment. She looked around the room.

"I think it's working, Bear," Mrs. Duck whispered.

"Come over here so she can see you."

Bear stood right in front of Roly-Poly and sang his song again.

Roly-Poly smiled a big smile, and she began to squirm.

"She wants you to hold her," said Mrs. Duck.
"She's too heavy," Bear said. "She squishes me, but I can sit beside her."
Mrs. Duck propped Roly-Poly up next to him.
Bear tickled Roly-Poly on the tummy, and his baby sister laughed.
Bear told Roly-Poly a story, and she listened.
"Now what?" said Mrs. Duck. "She doesn't look very sleepy."

"Let's give her a bath," said Bear.
So Bear and Mrs. Duck lifted Roly-Poly into the bathtub.

Then they climbed in too. Roly-Poly let Mrs. Duck hold her, but she wanted *Bear* to push the toy boat to her. And she wanted *Bear* to dry her off with the towel.

And she wanted *Bear* to tuck her into bed and sing her to sleep.

BABY BEAR

Suddenly the front door banged open and Nora came into the room

"I'm home," Nora said.

"SHHHHHHH," said Bear.

"How did you get her to sleep?" Nora whispered.

"Bear did," said Mrs. Duck.

"Roly-Poly's lucky to have an older brother like you," said Nora.

Bear smiled. "I want to be near her when she wakes up."

He pushed his bed next to Roly-Poly's. He leaned over and gave his baby sister a tiny kiss.

"Good night," he whispered.

Then he climbed into bed and closed his eyes.